Alvin Lincoln Snow

Songs of the white Mountains and other Poems

Alvin Lincoln Snow

Songs of the white Mountains and other Poems

ISBN/EAN: 9783743337107

Manufactured in Europe, USA, Canada, Australia, Japa

Cover: Foto ©Andreas Hilbeck / pixelio.de

Manufactured and distributed by brebook publishing software
(www.brebook.com)

Alvin Lincoln Snow

Songs of the white Mountains and other Poems

SONGS

OF THE

WHITE MOUNTAINS

AND

OTHER POEMS,

BY

ALVIN L. SNOW.

———— ——

CRESTON, IOWA:
THE GAZETTE PUBLISHING HOUSE.
1892.

☀CONTENTS☀

QUATRAINS:—

Contents.

SONGS

OF THE

WHITE MOUNTAINS.

Songs of the White Mountains.

— -

PROEM.

I loathe the city, with its ceaseless whirl
    And din and turbulence! I love the green,
Gay country, with its sparkling streams that purl
    Down wooded glens and grassy valleys serene—
I love the sylvan and the mountainous scene!
    O, let me leave dull streets and crowds behind;
Let leagues of flowery landscape intervene
    Between me and the halls to Pride assigned,
And let me gaze on earth with meditative mind!

O, ye grand Peaks that nobly tower above
    All others in your region, as did those
Whose names ye bear, whose memories we love,
    Tower in their time o'er mightiest friends and foes!
When Summer's hand your cold white mantles throws
    Aside, and wraps ye in rich robes of green,
And decks your bosoms with the glowing rose,
    What joy to scale your heights sublime, serene,
And like some eagle view the circumambient scene!

Gladly I leave the city and its strife,
 Gladly your solitudes, O, Mountains, seek,
Where liberty and peace and joy are rife!
 Hail—hail to thee, O, thou world-famous Peak!
The rolling centuries have not made thee weak;
 Thou art as when the sun first looked on thee,
Giant of Nature!   Tempests dire may wreak
 Their fury on earth, and men may cease to be,—
Thou standest firm as God's unalterable decree!

ODE TO MOUNT WASHINGTON.

I.

O, Peak, with thy stony splinters,
    And pine-fringed granite bed!
The flakes of a thousand winters
    Have plumed thy lofty head!
And thou seem'st now, to the bard,
    A warrior brave and old,
And thou seem'st the land to guard,
    With aspect proud and bold!

II.

Heard'st thou that anthem which rang
    So rapturously o'er earth—
That pæan the Stars of Morning sang,
    To hail the young World's birth?
Thou hast naught wherewith to speak,
    And yet I fancy thou hast
A voice, O, veteran Peak!
    Which tells of periods past.

III.

When silence profound—unbroken—
    Around thee reigned of yore,
And the ambient wilds no token—
    No trace of mortals bore—
Ere Man, in admiration,
    First saw thee pierce the skies,
Didst thou dream of the puissant Nation
    That 'neath thy glance should rise?

IV.

Most noble art thou—transcendent
    In name and fame thou art!
Thy name—ah, how resplendent,
    How sacred to the heart
That name!—Ere thou wast christened,
    O, Mount! that NAME so grand
With Fame's own halo glistened,
    On pages of our land.

V.

Fair Right rose bravely to wreak
    Just vengeance upon foul Wrong;
And hoar Oppression waxed weak,
    And youthful Freedom grew strong.
The weapon Heaven hallowed that hour
    To the Hero of Heroes was given;
He severed the gyves of Power—
    By him were our Land's fetters riven.

VI.

O, deem it sacred dust,
    And worthy of highest renown,
Where sleeps the Wise and Just,
    Who trampled the Tyrant down,
Ye millions!—ye that are now,
    And ye millions that yet are to be!—
With reverence bare the brow
    At the Shrine of the mighty and free!

VII.

We come from a Father's Tomb,
    And see in the Mount sublime
A symbol of HIM to whom
    Our Land owes its golden prime!
Ah, reverently breathe we that name—
    The name of our Nation's Sire!
Thou recordest none, O, Fame!
    Purer or nobler or higher.

VIII.

Stand in thy peerless glory,
    O, Chief of the Northern Hills!
Cleansed are the fields once gory;
    Sweet Peace her mission fulfills:
Oppression no more hath entry—
    Blest Liberty hath sole sway!
Stand—stand like a stalwart sentry—
    O, proudly stand for aye!—

IX.

Stand while Earth's generations
    Come forth and like the grass
Fade—whilst with their mutations
    The flying centuries pass:—
As erst, with brow unbent,
    Still tower erect and free!
Thou art his best monument
    Whose name is given to thee!

AMONG THE MOUNTAINS.

O, ye eternal Mountains!
　How gloriously ye stand!
How sweet your argent fountains!
　Your stately forms how grand!

Avaunt, O, wraith-like Sorrow!
　O, phantom Care, depart!
Go, dark thoughts of to-morrow!
　Be lightsome, O, my heart!

At will I here may wander,
　Unvexed by the city's strife;
Alone I here may ponder
　On Nature and Nature's life!

O, ye who 'mid Art's treasured
　Works rove, her halls forsake!
In Nature's realm unmeasured
　Your thirst for grandeur slake!

Leave, leave cold imitations
　Of the beautiful and sublime—
Ephemeral creations
　Effaced by scoffing Time!—

Come, view these Heights eternal!
　On Nature's glories gaze—
Glories that seem Supernal,
　In these halcyon Summer days!

SUNRISE.

The East is a sheet of silver,
  The West is sullenly gray;—
A glow on the distant mountain-tops
  Announces the coming day.

A cloud o'er yon wild Peak hovers—
  It is changed to a crimson robe—
Lo! the Sun, in imperial splendor,
  Looks o'er the awakening globe!

MOUNTAIN SCENES.

How sweet in the radiant Summer days
  (And not in Summer only)
On these sublimest scenes to gaze!
  Oh, who can here be lonely?

What joy to wander all day long,
  In golden hours of leisure,
Far from the tumult and the throng,
  With Nature—ay, what pleasure!

Turn where thou wilt, what wonders rise—
  Marvels beyond thy dreaming!
Here rove and feast thy ravished eyes,
  Thyself in Paradise deeming!

Ah, scenes unrivaled!—Thou mayst stray,
  O, wanderer bold and fearless,
O'er all the world, yet thou wilt say
  These glorious scenes are peerless!

THE MOUNTAIN RETREAT.

Away from the ceaseless turmoil,
  Away from the dust and heat,
How pleasant to rest on the earth's green breast,
  In this cool and quiet retreat!

Away from the mocking splendors,
  And the vanities numberless,
Of Fashion's train and Mammon's reign—
  From the multitude's throng and press!

Away from crowded structures,
  And the ways by myriads trod,
In Nature's home, 'neath Heaven's own dome,
  Alone 'mid the works of God!

O, most delightful rambles,
  O, most delicious dreams,
On mountain-brows—under verdant boughs
  —Beside pellucid streams!

'Tis a foretaste of Elysium—
  Of the joys the Blessed know!
Oh! there is not a sweeter spot
  In the wide, wide world below!

MOONRISE ON MOUNT WASHINGTON.

Upon this Titan Height all eyes
Are centered on the eastern skies,
To watch the moon's bright orb arise.

She comes—fair Luna comes; for, lo!
The far horizon is aglow
With silver radiance which doth grow!

Behold her rim of argent sheen!—
Behold the grand Nocturnal Queen,
In all her majesty serene!

How gloriously she throws her beams
O'er vales and heights, o'er woods and streams!
How wondrous beautiful she seems!

As higher up yon sky she soars,
What splendor upon earth she pours!—
Glory like that from Heaven's own doors!

How her rays so clear and strong
Silver o'er the enchanted throng!
Oh, scene to be remembered long!

IN THE GLEN.

A tiny brook meanders down the glen—
  An argent streamlet musical and fleet;
  I love to listen to its murmuring sweet—
Have hearkened to it hour by hour.   O, when
I grow aweary of the haunts of men,
  I seek within its depths a quiet retreat,
  Where overhead the whispering branches meet,
And, waiving care, I am most happy then.
O, tranquil glen! O, pure, melodious brook!
  How much of earthly bliss to you I owe!
  The busy world may deem you dull indeed;
Little I reck.   Give me my favorite nook,
  And that soft rippling! Lonely I cannot grow—
  For aught more pleasurable I will not plead.

NOONTIDE.

No lightsome breeze is floating now;
The trees on each Peak's lofty brow
Like silent, motionless sentries stand,
Looking o'er the mountain land.

How tranquil is the hour!   No sound
Steals from the solitudes around:
Bird of song and bird of prey
To deepest shades have stolen away.

Dazzlingly the sun looks down
On each Height's gigantic crown—
Into glens and gorges deep:—
'Neath his rays earth seems asleep.

ECHO LAKE.

Here softly blow thy bugle.—
    What wild, sweet sounds awake!—
What echoes—heavenly echoes—
    Float over Echo Lake!

Listen—O, listen—listen!
    How sweet beyond compare!—
Each note dissolves in sweetness
    On the enchanted air!

How clear and bright the waters!
    How sweetly the ripples play!—
On this beautiful sheet of silver,
    Let us gently launch away!

Ah! gracefully as the swallow
    Wings his rapid flight,
Over this matchless mirror
    Speeds our boat so light!

Once more lift up thy bugle—
    The dreamy silence break!
O, sounds—O, visions of Heaven!
    O, peerless Echo Lake!

THE SILVER CASCADE.

O, nowhere, save in Heaven,
  Is there a lovelier stream—
Not even in the enchanting
  Eden of a dream!

Nowhere in all the regions
  By mortal eyes surveyed
May be seen a torrent so beautiful
  As thine, O, argent Cascade!

Ah! sweeter, wilder music
  Ne'er made Man's soul rejoice
Than the sempiternal melody
  Of thy never-silent voice!

I gaze and gaze upon thee,
  And hearken, hearken long,
Entranced by thy magic loveliness,
  And the witchery of thy song!

Flow on, flow on forever,
  Descending from on high,
In thy beauty and sweetness and purity,
  Like an angel from the sky.

MOONLIGHT ON THE HEIGHTS.

The full-orbed moon ascends the sky,
And looks serenely from on high:
How softly her rays of silver rest
On each majestic mountain's crest !

Alone, in musing mood, I stand
Upon this Height so wild, so grand,
And bare my brow to feel the light
Caress of the cool wind of night.

How beautiful, how quiet is all
Around, below, above !—The fall
Of some sweet fount soft melody makes—
No other sound the stillness breaks.

As tranquilly, O, Orb serene,
Didst thou look down upon this scene
—On these Peaks so high and vast,
In unnumbered centuries past.

Long ages hence, when all who gaze
On thee shall walk no more earth's ways,
Those wilt as placidly look down,
And these famed Heights with radiance crown.

THE WIND AMONG THE PINES.

Like the murmur of the ocean,
　As its waves in endless lines
Seek the shore with rolling motion,
　Sounds the wind among the pines!

O'er the emerald-mantled mountains,
　Drowning—overpowering quite
The silver voices of the fountains,
　It rushes with its breath of might.

Close thine eyes—a moment darken
　Thy vision—let thy fancy reign:—
Thou dost deem, as thou dost hearken,
　Thou standest by the mighty main:—

Thou dost dream of vessels speeding
　Unto many a far-off land,
In distance lessening—fast receding
　O'er the sweep of waters grand;—

Thou dost dream of sunny highlands,
　On whose tall cliffs white surges beat,—
Of reefs of coral—wave-kissed islands
　Ever romantic, ever sweet;—

Thou dost dream of caves enchanted,
　Where many a songful mermaid dwells,—
Of shores where sirens erst descanted—
　Of beaches strewn with rose-lipped shells!

Blissful dreaming—radiant vision!
  But cease thy revery—ope thine eyes:—
Behold these bowers that seem Elysian—
  These Peaks that soar to cloudless skies!

Scenes as nobly grand as Ocean's
  Thou viewest with admiring gaze—
As lofty, as sublime emotions
  In thy enraptured soul they raise.

Ah! thrilling as the shout victorious
  Of a conquering army's lines
Is the sound, forever glorious,
  Of the wind among the pines!

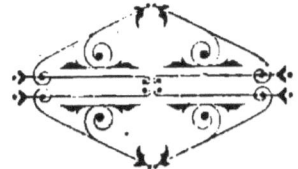

THE MOUNTAIN STORM.

A low and ominous rumble
    Steals from the distant west;—
Lo! a cloud black and dread lifts its demon-like head
    Over yon mountain's crest!

Quickly—ah, how quickly
    The heavens are with gloom o'erspread!
Anon huge drops bespatter the tops
    Of the pine-trees overhead.

Now behold! in all its fury
    The Summer shower comes down;
And the rolling thunder shakes all things under
    The Storm-fiend's ebon frown!

More fiercely fall the torrents,
    And dimmer grows the day;
While with dazzling flash and horrific crash
    The lightnings and thunders play.

Hearken!   A sound appalling!—
    A most heavy and sullen shock!
Ah! a lurid dart hath riven the heart
    Of a pine on yon tower of rock!

In the vales the streamlets are roaring
    Like rivers in their pride;   [nooks
Rills swollen to brooks course through lightning-lit
    Adown each mountain's side!

But see! In the western heaven
Shines the blue sky of day!
The lightnings red and the thunders dread
Move farther and farther away!

'Tis past—and all is peaceful!
The smiling sun looks down,
With its wonted glow, upon all below;—
How it gilds each proud Peak's crown!

SUNSET.

Beyond yon giant Height the sun
Hath passed in all his glory;—
The West is as red as a battle-field gory!
The Summer day is done.

Paler, paler grows the sky,
Where Daylight's parting hues
Their magical radiance diffuse—
They fade—alas, they die!

Each tint—each glowing tint is gone!
The West is robed in gray:
The Peaks—ah, phantom-like are they,
As the shades of Night steal on.

FAREWELL TO THE MOUNTAINS.

Farewell, O, ye Mountains—ye Noblest of Mountains!
　Farewell to your bowers—ah, sweetest of bowers!
Farewell to your fountains—most musical fountains!
　Farewell to your flowers—most beautiful flowers!
No more shall I hail the glad advent of Morning,
　On your crests that tow'rd Heaven in such majesty swell;
Nor when Sunset's gay fires, your proud spires adorning,
　Flame forth shall I view you, O, Mountains!—Farewell!

Farewell, ye grand Mountains! with exquisite pleasure
　I have wandered among you in loveliest days—
Ah, the joys of those days my remembrance shall treasure!
　In fancy full oft on your scenes I shall gaze—
Often, yea, often in sweet retrospection
　Each ravishing scene, each loved spot I shall view!
Oh, ne'er can you fade from my soul's recollection,
　Ye Mountains—ye glorious Mountains!—Adieu!

Farewell—ay, farewell!   From the pine-tree's soft rustle,
　The murmur of brooklets and wild-birds' sweet songs,
I must haste to the city's commotion and bustle,
　Its wearisome hum and its vast surging throngs.
But where'er I may be, though oft burdened with sadness,
　Wherever in all the wide world I may dwell,
Fond Mem'ry shall ever revert with true gladness
　To my stay in your midst, sublime Mountains!—Farewell!

OTHER POEMS.

OTHER POEMS.

— — —— — —

TROUBLE.

O, why be ever watching
  For ills and woes to come?
Why brood o'er days that are to be,
  And evermore be glum?
Press on, press on! With courage
  Your way in life pursue,
And pay no heed to trouble
  Till trouble comes to you.

The sun is brightly shining,
  Although the heavens frown;
And soon the clouds will fall apart,
  And radiance will come down.
O, keep a brave heart ever,
  And have a prize in view,
And pay no heed to trouble
  Till trouble comes to you.

The past is past forever;
　And why should we recall
Its bygone cares, its vanished griefs?
　O, strive to banish all!
Wait cheerfully the future,
　Take heart and hope anew,
And pay no heed to trouble
　Till trouble comes to you.

The bird that sings so sweetly
　Upon the greenwood spray
Dreams not of darksome days to come—
　Is happy in to-day.
Each life must have its trials,
　And yours may not be few,
But pay no heed to trouble
　Till trouble comes to you.

Our merciful Creator
　Is wiser far than we,
And what is best for every one
　Unerringly can see.
O, look to Him and trust Him,
　And He will guide you through
All perils.　HEED NOT TROUBLE
　TILL TROUBLE COMES TO YOU.

LOVE.

You may seek for earthly treasure,
  Vast wealth you may obtain;
You may taste what the world calls pleasure,
  High honor you may gain:
You may dwell 'neath the brightest skies
  That ever smiled above,
But you ne'er will be happy, though rich or wise,
  Without the boon called love.

You may roam the wide world over,
  You may journey o'er land and sea,
But vain, O, restless rover,
  Will all your wanderings be.
You will be, in every land,
  Like a weary and homeless dove;
You will ne'er be content, though 'mid scenes most grand,
  If you have not the treasure love.

You may pave your way to glory
  With victories nobly won;
Your name may shine in story,
  In fame be surpassed by none:
But you ne'er will be satisfied,
  If you have not something above
The blare of renown—above pomp and pride—
  And that precious something is love.

O, Love! 'tis thy blest chalice
   That makes life sweet to all,
In cottage or in palace,
   Where'er the sun's rays fall.
Still gladden every shore,
   Thou benison from above!
Oh! rule in our hearts forevermore,
   Pure, Heaven-sent, glorious Love!

WHEN THE SWEETEST SONGS ARE SUNG.

'Tis not when our souls are fraught
   With the fanciful and the ideal,
But when, in sober thought,
   They dwell on the true and the real.

The heart's depths must be stirred,
   Ere song's full tide can roll,—
Ere the poet can pen a magical word,
   Or the minstrel charm a soul.

CLIMB HIGH!

--

"There is always room at the top."   WEBSTER.

Wouldst thou win, upon the earth,
   Fame that shall not die?
A widespread name—a name of worth?
      Climb high!

Let no task dismay thy soul;
   With the noblest vie:
Strive to reach a lofty goal;
      Climb high!

Let not languor o'er thee steal;
   O'er no lost hope sigh:
Arduous work demands thy zeal;
      Climb high!

Science is a towering peak;
   To scale it wouldst though try?
Dauntlessly its summit seek;
      Climb high!

Wouldst thou sing immortal lays?
   Wouldst thou glorify
The world of song—evoke its praise?
      Climb high!

Wouldst thou gain earth's glittering gold?
Fortune will not deny
The boon—be resolute and bold;
    Climb high!

Wouldst thou nobler make the world?
Bid Error pale and fly?
With the flag of Truth unfurled,
    Climb high!

Upward! Upward! Does thy way
'Mid thorny labyrinths lie?
Turn not back—press forward aye;
    Climb high!

Upward, upward evermore!
Time glides swiftly by;
Dare and do ere life be o'er:
    Climb high!

O, shrink not from life's heaviest cross!
All earthly ills defy;
Be not o'ercome by woe or loss:
    Climb high!

Do clouds of disappointment dark
Sweep across thy sky?
A Voice from Heaven shall cheer thee—hark!
    "Climb High!"

Upward, upward lift thy soul:
Upward turn thine eye:
Seek the grand Eternal Goal;
    CLIMB HIGH!

THAT SUMMER BESIDE THE SEA.

Bright Summer is smiling once more,
   Her cloudless sky is o'erhead,
But I ramble not on the shore
   Where Pleasure's votaries tread.
The billows, as they rise and sink,
   Make no more their murmurs to me;
Alone I walk, alone I think
   Of a Summer beside the sea—
   Of a Summer dead and gone by the sea.

A snowy and rose-lipped shell
   I hold within my hand,
And seem to see surges swell,
   And hear them smite the sand.
But I will gather shells no more;
   For sundered for aye are we
Who strayed together on the shore
   That Summer beside the sea,—
   That Summer dead and gone by the sea.

But I dream of another sea,—
   I dream of another shore,
Where the soul from earth's pangs is free—
   Where hearts are severed no more.
Ah ! somewhere on that winterless Strand
   Where blooms Life's fadeless Tree,
When Truth's vail is rent, we may understand
   Each other—beside that Sea—
   That eternal Supernal Sea.

THE MAELSTROM.

O, there is a gulf in a far-off deep,
Whose whirling waters never sleep !
Horridly swirling round and round,
They appall the ear with their mighty sound !
Ever and aye, by night and by day,
They revel in wild, infernal play.
Ah ! woe to the cautionless, luckless ship
That ventures near the monster's lip:
Woe if she floateth beyond the verge:
Naught mortal can save her—she cannot emerge—
She is lost in the Hell of the circling surge.

There is a Maelstrom in every clime,
Whose wrecks, alas ! are souls sublime.
Whirled in its terrible grasp they go
Down to the depths of eternal woe.
·It swirleth, swirleth night and day,
It whirleth, whirleth aye and aye.
Millions into its gulf are borne,
Millions are lost and millions mourn !
It rages, rages and spurns control.
This destroyer of the soul
Is the stream that flows from the maddening bowl.

ONWARD!

Onward! Let this be our motto,
　And the burden of our song!
With the word upon our banners,
　Let us bravely march along!
Onward! there are fields of glory
　We may win by noble strife;
Waste no time in idle dreaming!
　Onward in the march of life!

Onward, onward! Ever onward!
　Look not back, nor stay thy feet;
Loiter not 'mid morning's freshness,
　Falter not 'mid noontide's heat.
Ever onward, ever onward!
　There are treasures to be won;
Haste to grasp them, lest they vanish
　Ere shall rise to-morrow's sun.

Onward! brighter days are coming,
　O, ye weary ones who toil!
Onward, laborer, grandly onward!
　From no worthy task recoil.
Onward, brilliant son of Genius!
　Honor waits thee—deathless fame!
Onward, onward to achievement!
　Thine may be a lofty name.

Onward! there are deeds of grandeur,
  Deeds of wonder to perform!
There are mighty hosts to vanquish,
  Towering fortresses to storm!
There are vast unfathomed problems
  In the boundless realm of Thought.
Onward, onward! You may solve them!
  Onward! Toil where none have wrought.

Onward in the ranks of Progress!
  O, let naught thy steps impede —
On with unremitting ardor!
  Never from the van recede!
All that makes Earth happier, better,
  All that elevates Mankind,
Strive with dauntless soul to forward!
  Not an instant fall behind.

Onward —on! Though worn and weary,
  Do not fail to render aid
To the struggling ones around you.
  Onward! Never be dismayed!
Onward in life's glorious battle,
  Though by foes most sorely pressed;
Onward! there is naught like courage!
  Victory brings joy and rest.

Onward ever, onward ever
  In the sacred cause of Right!
Let not Error's threats alarm thee,
  Though her arm is full of might.
Onward! If thou be triumphant,
  Thou shalt wear a peerless crown;

Thou shalt share the bliss of angels!
Onward! heed not scoff nor frown.

Onward, though the way be thorny;
On tow'rd Heaven! on tow'rd God!
Onward till you scale the Mountains
That no mortal feet have trod!
Onward till by Life's pure River
You may rest—the bright Goal won—
And the sweet voice of the Master
Shall repeat the words, "WELL DONE!"

EULOGY— PRESIDENT GARFIELD.

(Read before the S. C. I. Society, Simpson College, October, 1881.)

Who are the wise? Go, light thine evening taper!
  Over the leaves of mighty volumes pore,
On words that speak to thee from lifeless paper
  Of those who've viewed the Universe before.
  Lo, he was wise who erst was wont to soar
Into the sky of soul—the sphere of Thought—
  The shining peaks of Knowledge to explore;
Who traced her dictates, unperplexed by aught,
And issued them anew, with added meaning fraught.

Who are the noble? Turn to grateful hearts,
  The glory of nobility to learn,
For gladdened lives are unto us as charts,
  Whereby their spirits' broadness we discern.
  Lo, he was noble who was wont to spurn
The lures of Wantonness and Ease, and go
  With succor to the hearth where ceased to burn
The last pale ember by the couch of Woe,
Establish comfort there and light anew its glow.

Like these, I ween, the wise and noble are.
  The traits of both united in one soul,
Which was our Country's lofty leading star.
  But unpent grief assumes a long control!
  That soul has flown, and Earth from pole to pole

Laments its flight untimely:—on that day
  When ruthlessly the dread Destroyer stole
The link that bound it to its native clay,
She mourned that her admired should thus be spurned away.

Our Country sitteth like a matron bowed
  In boundless sorrow for her true Knight slain;
And the surrounding nations like a crowd
  Of sisters sympathize—and not in vain
  Their tears with hers have mingled like the rain,
And hallowed Justice calls for that base one,
  Whom all that breathe with high contempt disdain,
By whom the deed—ignoble deed—was done,
Which early hath entombed fair Freedom's favorite son.

Vain-minded Guiteau! thou hast won a fame
  Dark as the blackness of the rayless night.
Thy name shall live—not like that better name
  Now sadly glorious to all human sight,
  But different as the dark is from the light—
On History's leaf, by Truth recorded there.
  Beneath HIS virtue she thy shame shall write,
Thy memory, like a stench, disgust shall bear,
And thou art doomed to walk with demons in despair.

Immortal GARFIELD! endlessly revered
  Thy name shall be—thou deathless in thy fall!
The monument thou to thyself hast reared
  By thy pure life more potent is than all
  Can make to thee who form the marble wall.
Thy deeds were thy best laurels.   Mighty man!
  With pleasure we thy words and acts recall!
Thy memory, through all Time's future span,
Shall be as fragrance.   Rest as but the holy can.

OUR BEAUTIFUL FLAG:

A NATIONAL ODE.

I.

O, beautiful Flag of our Nation!
  The Banner of Banners thou art,
Fair Standard!—the world's admiration,
  The pride of the patriot's heart!
Thou wearest the crimson of morning,
  Heaven's blue and the hue of the snow,
And the bright stars of Heaven adorning
  Thy folds—how sublimely they glow!

II.

Wave forever, O, Banner of Beauty!
  Forevermore wave—freely wave!
To revere thee is life's sweetest duty,
  To defend thee the joy of the brave!
Over land, over ocean victorious,
  Float for aye, kissed by Heaven's golden light,
O, Standard of standards most glorious,
  O, symbol of freedom and might!

III.

O, beautiful Flag of our Nation!
  How bravely the noble and good,
'Neath the Stars of thy grand Constellation,
  In defence of our Country have stood!

How brilliant thy triumphs on ocean,
  Thy conquests on battle-swept field!
To thee our most loyal devotion,
  Our hearts' deepest homage we yield!

IV.

Oh! when the wild battle is raging,
  How sweet to behold thee above,
The rapture of vict'ry presaging,
  Fair Flag of our hope and our love!
Like angels' eyes tenderly beaming,
  Thy sweet Stars look down on the dead;
Like a seraph's wing radiantly streaming,
  Thou flutterest softly o'erhead!

V.

When traitors dared basely and madly
  Thy orient fabric to rend,
What heroes rose nobly and gladly
  Thy Stars and thy Stripes to defend!
Peace reigns where the cannon roared loudly,
  And hostile ranks bristled with steel;
Thy colors fly gayly and proudly,
  And all hearts are true to thy weal.

VI.

O, beautiful Flag of our Nation!
  We uphold thee with heart and with hand;
For thy glory and thy preservation
  Until death we would dauntlessly stand!
Every enemy's ensign before thee
  Shall go down with a meteor's flight,
And Heaven smile approvingly o'er thee
  When proud foes are vanquished in fight!

VII.

Flag of Freedom —blest Flag of our Nation!
  Bright Banner of peerless renown!
May the orbs of thy proud Constellation,
  Thy heavenly Stars, ne'er go down!
In peace, or 'mid war wild and gory,
  Stream in splendor and triumph above!
We pledge thee, O, Banner of Glory!
  Everlasting allegiance and love.

ON THE BATTLE-FIELD OF SARATOGA.

Ah! here a great triumph for Freedom
        Was won,
In that Conflict which made us a Nation—
  The grandest under the sun!

Here the haughty and bold British Lion
        Recoiled
Before the brave swoop of our Eagle--
  Here an arrogant foeman was foiled!

Here was vanquished the host of Oppression!
        For aye
Be this field and its heroes remembered,
  And the victory gained in that fray!

THE SUNSET BIRD.

There is a bird in Alaska which sings only at sunset, and which is therefore
called the Sunset Bird.

In a far-off land of cold and snow
  Sings the beautiful Sunset Bird;
And only in sunset's golden glow
  Its wonderful song is heard.
Not in broad day, when other birds sing,
Making the depths of wild woods ring,
But when the sun doth its last rays fling
By his exquisite marvellous carolling
  The solitudes are stirred.

He sings of the grandeur of earth and sky,
  The glories of even-time,
When the wandering winds so softly sigh,
  And the stars the heavens climb.
As departing Day bids the world adieu—
As shines each gorgeous sunset hue
In the western heaven so deeply blue,
Floateth his strain the dark wood through,
  Enchanting and sublime.

'Tis a lullaby for the weary earth,
  A song of peace and rest;
And more of solace than of mirth
  Is by those notes expressed.
O, songster rare, O, songster rare!
Few may hear thy magic air.
Would that mortal songs could share
The witchery thy lay doth bear,
  Its sweetness and its zest!

EASTER PÆAN.

O, bells, ring joyously and long!
O, Earth, break forth in grateful song!
Right hath triumphed over Wrong—
    Rent is the tomb's dark prison!
The Crucified, the Crucified
For us Heaven's gates hath opened wide!
For our guilty souls He died—
    Christ is risen!

No more shall Man in hopeless woe
Pass this mortal life below!
Blow, ye fragrant lilies, blow!
    Burst is the tomb's dark prison!
He whose blood for us was spilt
Hath atoned for all our guilt!
O, World, be jubilant! Yea, thou wilt—
    Christ is risen!

He who bore our weight of sin
Lies no longer cold within
Earth's bosom. Angels here have been—
    Unsealed the tomb's dark prison!
He liveth! ne'er again to die!
He reigneth! throned with God on high!
Let praise like incense fill the sky—
    Christ is risen!

A PSALM OF SPRING.

O, the merry, merry Spring-time,
　Has a charm for every eye!
For its lovely flowers and blossoms,
　And its sunny bright-blue sky,
And its gayly-warbling songsters,
　And its murm'ring silv'ry streams,
A rapture bring to Fancy,
　Like sweet pictures in our dreams!

O, the brightness of the Spring-time,
　When the darksome days are past,
And the pall-like clouds of Winter
　O'er the earth no more are cast!
How we love the vernal sunshine,
　With its warm reviving ray,
Bringing life and bloom and gladness—
　Driving gloom and grief away!

O, the music of the Spring-time!
　How it calls to mind the lays
That we sang amid the freshness
　Of our Youth's gay Spring-time days!
To the Fairy-land of Childhood
　How it calls our memories back!
Ah! we bask among the visions
　Of our life's bright early track!

O, the joyous days of Spring-time,
    They are sweetest of the year!
May we well know how to prize them,
    For their beauty and their cheer!
Let us praise the glorious Giver,
    And be thankful while we sing,
For the blessings and rejoicings
    Of another happy Spring!

AFTER THE STORM.

Last night the storm in its fury fell;
    Beneath its horrid frown,
Earth seemed for a brief while changed to Hell,
    And torrents came fiercely down—
    In a mad, wild rush came down.

But lo! how sweetly doth Morning smile!
    She is like an angel bright,
Whom naught can make sorrowful, naught defile!
    The storm, like a demon sprite,
Has passed. Earth is peaceful. The air breathes balm,
The sky is azure, the sea is calm.

THE VIOLETS.

I miss them in the valley,
  I miss them by the brook,
Whose quiet waters dally
  In many a lovely nook,
I miss them on the velvety lawn;
  I miss them on the rugged mount—
  I miss them by the murmuring fount—
Alas! the violets are gone.

Why should I heed the going
  Of such an humble flower?
Flowers far more showy are blowing
  Around me every hour—
Flowers radiant—roseate as the dawn—
  Flowers white and dazzling as the snow—
  Flowers golden as the sun's own glow—
Alas! the violets are gone.

I love them, O, I love them,
  Those flowers that wear the hue
Of the pure heavens above them—
  Most sweetly, mildly blue!
Though flowers more splendid smile upon
  This globe of ours—flowers gorgeous—grand—
  Dear are those blossoms meek and bland.
Alas! the violets are gone.

AT PARTING.

As the years—rapid years—move onward—
  As the years—changeful years—go by,
May my mem'ry to thee be ever
  Like a star in a tranquil sky.

We shall meet—ah, never, never,
  (Save in the Land of Dreams)
Till we rove in Regions Supernal,
  Beside eternal streams.

Words—sighs—tears—all are fruitless—
  The cup cannot from us pass;
We may not shun—we must quaff it—
  Most bitter cup, alas!

It *must* be—we must sever;
  But *thy* mem'ry aye shall be
Like the sun, in splendor shining
  On my way across Life's Sea.

FLOWERS.

The world is besprinkled with flowers—
Flowers fragrant, unsullied and sweet;
They bloom where the mountain towers,
They bloom in the vale at my feet.
The flowers that my love loved best
Are around me everywhere,
But, alas! she will wear them no more on her breast,
Nor entwined with her gold-hued hair.

O, flowers! she worshipped your hues, —
She adored your exquisite breath!
All lonely I wander and muse
On the mystery men call death.
Her cheeks are robbed of their bloom—
She slumbers in earth's cold breast!—
I scatter, with tears, on the turf of her tomb
The flowers that my love loved best!

THE CITY BY THE SEA.

O, splendid was that City—
That vast and marvellous City!
Most gorgeous were its palaces—most lofty its towers and
spires—
Its temples vast and glorious—
Its bannered hosts victorious—
There poets sang sublimely—noble minstrels touched their
lyres!

But upon that stately City
(Oh, who wept not in deepest pity?)
A terrible doom—a most horrible doom—an appalling doom
was sent!
Ah! Earth, so quiet, so slumbrous seeming,
Suddenly ceased placidly dreaming,
And muttered in wrath—trembled with wrath—with measure-
less wrath long pent!

With fiercely-heaving bosom, under
That fated City Earth spoke in thunder—
Like an ireful monster uttered a most loud and menacing
roar—
And, with rapid downward motion,
Made for wildly-sweeping Ocean
A bed whereon its billows dread should rest forevermore! .

And upon that queenly City—
Ah, that *too haughty* City!
Where abode the great and mighty, crowned with honors
manifold,
The Deep rushed in madness—
In maniacal gladness—
In demoniacal rapture o'er it furiously rolled!

Sank those palaces domed and golden—
Sank those temples huge and olden—
Sank—forever sank that City, far-famed, storied, powerful,
grand!
The waters—ruthless waters! gleaming
Above it tranquilly are dreaming.
Desolate—ay, most desolate is that erst most populous strand!

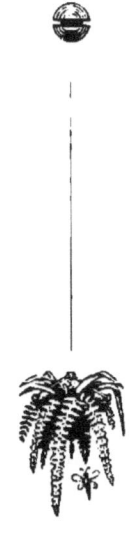

O, THE LILIES!

O, the lilies, the beautiful lilies,
    The lilies that bloom in the field!
What lessons, what glorious lessons,
    What marvellous lessons they yield—
What lessons of infinite wisdom
    By them unto Man are revealed!

O, the lilies, the odorous lilies,
    The lilies that float on the lake!—
Snowy lilies, immaculate lilies,
    Which the blue wavelets laughingly shake—
Lilies white as the robes of the angels!—
    What rapture in us they awake!

O, the lilies, the orient lilies,
    The lilies that deck the parterre!—
Gay lilies, magnificent lilies,
    Lilies gaudy—most gorgeous—most rare—
Oh! no potentate, throned, crowned and sceptred,
    Ever shone in such garb as they wear!

O, lilies, profoundly sage lilies,
    How sweet is the lore that you teach!
O, lilies, O, eloquent lilies,
    How grand are the sermons you preach!
How sublime, how soul-stirring your language—
    Your unworded, unspoken speech!

O, lilies, O, magical lilies!
  Still bloom—still enchantingly bloom!
Ah, worthy your mission—most noble!
  Ye banish our sadness and gloom:—
Ye remind us of Gardens unfading
  In Regions beyond the dread tomb.

QUATRAINS.

CONDOLENCE.

.

Sing me no lightsome ditty,
    Nor tell me all woe is brief;
They only know how to pity,
    Who have felt the self-same grief.

NEW SCENES.

.

Let the grim hermit dwell where none intrudes;
    I love new scenes with fresh enchantments rife:
He who hath passed through most vicissitudes
    Knows most of life.

SWEETEST OF ALL.

.

There are manifold things enchanting
    In Nature and in Art.
But the sweetest of all things earthly
    Is the love of a gentle heart.

BURDENS.

Bear ye one another's burdens:
  So fulfill the law of love.
Priceless crowns shall be your guerdons,
  In the Land of Rest above.

LINES WRITTEN IN AN ALBUM.

The flowers that bloom on the lea
  Will fade and will wither away,
But, Dear Friend! my remembrance of thee
  Can never grow dim or decay.

FROST-PICTURES.

Lo, there are wondrous pictures on my window-pane !
  Castles, with turrets rising grandly high,—
  Cities, with bright spires towering to the sky,
Like angel fingers pointing tow'rd Heaven's fair Domain.

UNDER BLUE SKIES.

Gayly we glide o'er Life's marvellous ocean!
  Beautiful prospects enchantingly rise:
Sweet is the voyage—safe and free from commotion—
      Under blue skies!

Royally, royally skim we the billows—
  O, grandly our bark o'er the sunny deep hies!
Bright thoughts glad our days and bright dreams bless our
    pillows,
      Under blue skies!

No peril arises—no evil betides us!
  Hope is our pilot—seraphic her guise—
Supernal her voice!—Ah, most sweetly she guides us,
      Under blue skies!

Woe—sable-browed Woe—we forevermore banish!
  What have we to do with dull weeping and sighs?
Avaunt, Care and Fear!—Like dim phantoms they vanish,
      Under blue skies!

With those whom we love and revere truly near us,—
  With all Love bestows—naught to us Love denies—
How much hath Existence to charm and to cheer us,
      Under blue skies!

O, fade not, thou Paradisiacal vision!
   Thou wilt not—thou wilt not!—still ravish our eyes!
We glide—let us doubt not—to regions Elysian,
         Under blue skies!

May the drear darksome cloud and the dread tempest never
   To menace our peace and enjoyment arise:
May our voyage on Life's main be henceforth, aye and ever,
         Under blue skies!

IN AUGUST.

A silver haze on the hills is lying;
  The ambient fields are like seas of gold:
Earth seems with regions Supernal vieing;
  Her beauties and glories are manifold.

But e'en 'mid the flush and blush of morning,
  E'en 'mid the glitter and glare of noon,
We catch a vague, yet real, warning
  Of sombre days that will come full soon;—

Of days when the flowers shall cease their blooming,
  And sweet-voiced songsters cease their lays,
When the golden sun, in gray skies glooming,
  Shall grudgingly yield his glorious rays;—

When the wandering winds shall sigh in sadness
  For the vanished splendors of earth and sky,
And, wilder growing, shall rave in madness,
  As bleaker, darker days draw nigh.

Ah, Autumn! soon wilt thou come hither!
  With fingers ruthless, frosty and cold,
Thou wilt touch the flowers—their forms will wither—
  Thou wilt make the landscape drear to behold.

Yet fondly, lovingly Summer dallies,
  Unwilling her joyous reign to cease,
While over the hills and over the valleys
  Broodeth a universal peace;—

A welcome quiet unmarred, unbroken,
  A sacred silence, a Sabbath calm,
A prayer unbreathed, a blessing unspoken,
  A solemnly beautiful wordless psalm.

O, when the Summer of life is fading,
  And soberer thoughts our minds engage,
May a calm as restful, our souls pervading,
  Herald the coming Autumn of Age!

PICTURES OF THE PAST.

I see them at dewy morning,
   I see them at glowing noon,
I see them at purple gloaming,
   And at night 'neath the argent moon;—
I see them at solemn midnight,
   In Dreamland's halls so vast,
Fair Memory's peerless paintings,
   Sweet pictures of the Past.

Naught can obscure the splendor
   Of a past day's cloudless sky.
To-day dark clouds may gather,
   Angry winds rush wildly by,
But in the scene before me
   There is neither cloud nor blast.
Nothing can dim the radiance
   Of this picture of the Past.

I gaze on orient flowers
   That ne'er can fade away,
On stately verdurous forests
   Whose leaves can ne'er decay;—
On sunny brows of beauty
   That grief can ne'er o'ercast.
O, naught excels in sweetness
   Fair pictures of the Past!

I gaze on silver rivers,
  I gaze on sapphire seas,
On lofty snow-crowned mountains,
  On far-extending leas;
On many a marvellous city,
  Magnificent and vast.
Ah, what a world of grandeur
  In pictures of the Past!

I see the olden, golden
  Haunts of sweet childhood days;
With what transcendent rapture
  On them once more I gaze!
The simple priceless treasures
  In those glad days amassed
Lie, as of yore, before me,
  In pictures of the Past!

Once more I see the loved ones
  Whose spirit-wings unfurled
Long, long since softly bore them
  Far, far above the world;
Once more their smiles of greeting
  As of old on me are cast.
Ah, blessed, ever blessed
  Are these pictures of the Past!

O, Memory, wondrous limner,
  With skill beyond compare!
Restore scenes olden—golden—
  Portray the pure and fair;—
Paint glorious, glorious pictures!
  Oh! long as life may last,
My soul shall view with fondness
  Sweet pictures of the Past!

LIFE.

A little of pleasure, a little of pain,
  A little of toil and of strife,
A little of sunshine, a little of rain,—
    Such is life!

A few fragile hopes and not a few fears,
  Anxiety evermore rife,
A few flitting smiles followed closely by tears,—
    Such is life!

A little of hate and a little of love—
  Bereavement that stabs like a knife—
Mournful eyes wistfully looking above—
    Such is life!

THE BY-GONE SUMMER.

The gardens are gorgeous with roses,
   Gay birds arc warbling rare lays;
Fair Nature her wealth discloses
   To Man's admiring gaze:
But something, alas! I miss from the earth,
   Something I miss from the sky;
I fruitlessly long for the music and mirth
   Of a beautiful Summer gone by!

The grandeur and the gladness
   Of the summer that smiles now
Can not dispel the sadness
   That clouds my heart and brow!
The heavens, perchance, are as blue and mild,
   And the roses as sweet to the eye,
Yet they seem not to me like those that smiled
   In that radiant Summer gone by.

O, days so full of sweetness—
   Of rare—most rare delight—
Ye sped with angels' fleetness!—
   O, days so bright—so bright—
My wishes can not restore your hours;
   I vainly, vainly sigh
For your faded rays and your perished flowers,
   O, glorious Summer gone by!

Ah, bygone Summer! thy glory
  Was enhanced by a lovely face;
Life's bloom was transitory—
  She lies in Earth's cold embrace!
I yearn for the clasp of a snowy hand—
  For the glance of a sapphire eye—
For the light of tresses thy soft winds fanned,
  O, wonderful Summer gone by!

Summers may come and vanish,
  With their fragrance and their bloom,—
Their splendor ne'er can banish
  My spirit's inmost gloom.
But be patient, my soul! Beyond earth's pain,
  In God's Summer-Land on high,
Where parting comes not, we may meet—we twain
  Who loved in that Summer gone by!

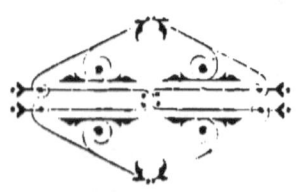

SONNET TO THE PYRAMIDS.

Grandly ye tower amid the desolate waste,
  Huge monuments of centuries gone by!
  While those who reared your forms forgotten lie—
Their history forevermore effaced.
Giants of Stone! By cloudless skies embraced,
  Ye rise so proudly, gloriously high,
  With earth's sublime, immovable peaks ye vie;
Like them ye stand and cannot be abased.
Cities have flourished and yielded to Decay;
  Empires have risen and fallen: surviving all,
    Ye look with scorn on evanescent things!
So shall ye stand till all things pass away—
  Yea, till this vast globe shall in fragments fall,
    Doomed to destruction by the King of Kings!

THE OASIS.

Lo, like an isle 'mid sombre sweep of sea,
   The green oasis in the desert lies!
   Here clearest fountains mirror clearest skies;
Here gracefully rises many an emerald tree,
Wherein gay songsters voice their guileless glee;
   Here the most ravishing flowers enchant mine eyes!
   Here smiling Nature bounteously supplies
All that man needs that he may happy be.
Behold! A caravan doth hither come!
With what delight the weary pilgrims hail
   This blessed spot! Long they yon waste have trod.
With joy o'ercome, their fevered lips are dumb!
They quaff the streams which never, never fail:—
   Anon their voices rise in thanks to God.

THE DESTROYED CITY.

There Opulence had his stately Hall,
    And Fashion her votaries gay;
Bounded by impregnable wall,
Loomed her palaces grand and tall.
(No foe could appall her—no forces enthrall her.)
In a moment—a flying moment—all,
    Mirage-like, melted away.

For the Mountain of Fire that soared far higher
    Than loftiest spire or tower,
Heaped tower and spire in a peerless pyre—
    Whelmed all in a burning shower.

With exultant roar, did the Demon out-pour
    The vials of his wrath,
And with his breath send woe and death
    To every mortal's path.

The Earthquake woke, and with sudden stroke
    Cleft the ghastly ruins in twain;
Wide gaped the earth and with hellish mirth
    Gulped down the fiery rain.

The palace proud and the hovel were bowed,
    And lay in one smouldering heap;
And the beggar-wight and the man of might
    Slept together the last long sleep.

Lofty and lowly (all sinful— none holy)
 Were plunged in a common tomb;
Youthful and old and craven and bold
 Alike met fearful doom.

And none escaped, wheresoe'er they shaped
 Their course,—ay, none could flee—   [them,
The raging earth shook them,---the fierce flame o'ertook
 And devoured them with horrible glee.

O, peacefully Morn came to adorn
 Peak, vale and ambient wood;
But her beams lit only a waste black and lonely
 Where late the vast City stood.

Ah, at the nod and beck of God
 The Mountain sent forth its flame;
And upon that City too vile for pity
 Heaven's righteous vengeance came.

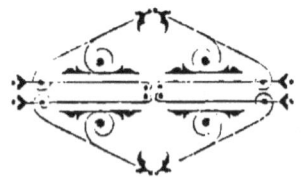

THE FALLING LEAVES.

The leaves are falling! Softly, one by one,
   They loose their hold on many a swaying limb,
   And, fluttering, drop amid the wood-aisles dim,
To lie obscure, uncomely, wrinkled, dun,
In spots damp, drear, unvisited by the sun.
   A dirge—a requiem—a most mournful hymn
   The wild winds voice above their untombed forms.
      Ah! grim
And pitiless Winter his prelude hath begun!
O, falling leaves!—Plaintive-voiced falling leaves!
Once ye were beauteous—now ye are not so;—
Once ye were gay—ye are no longer gay!
With you, in sympathy, Man's spirit grieves!
Ye call to mind a sad, sad truth we know,—
That earthly loveliness must pass away!

NOVEMBER.

The valley is filled with a sea of mist,
  The village lies submerged below;
Over its spires, no more sun-kissed,
  The sombre vapor-billows flow.
The world is desolate!   I have known
No gloomier day, among all that have flown.
The flowers are dead and the bare woods moan,
  For this is dreary November.

O, for a bright, reviving ray—
  O, for a glimpse of the sunlight's gold!
The sky is gray and the sea is gray,
  Gray is the landscape and drear to behold.
Wan Sadness comes with the cheerless hours,
Crosses the the threshold—haunts the bowers—
Ah! we sigh for the solace of sun and flowers,
  In cloudy, dreary November.

One thought is evoked by cloud and blast—
  By earth and sky in their garb of woe:—
Youth's sunny days will not always last,
  Nor Beauty's roses forever glow.
Every soul, however gay,
Must know full many a darksome day,
When youth and bloom shall have passed away—
  Each life must have its November.

THE HAUNTED MANSION.

Gloomy, but grand, it rises nobly high,
Amid huge emerald circumambient trees.
Fair vines, whose beautiful blossoms scent the breeze,
Clamber till on its very roof they lie.
Proudly its cupola points to the sky !
Round it lie lawns as smooth as summer seas;
Nature and Art are there combined to please,
But none will dwell within those walls or nigh.
All there seems dead till midnight's solemn hour,
And then (so gossiping villagers declare)
A mysterious light at one high window gleams;
And by that light a form is seen to cower
Like one in mortal terror or despair,
Then fade away—like those beheld in dreams.

THE CHIHUANDASSI.

There is a mountain in Mexico, upon whose spacious summit exists a vine which has the power of motion, and an invariable tendency quickly to approach and entwine itself about whatever happens to come near it. The natives have many traditions concerning it, and many travellers and adventurers are said to have perished by being caught and crushed by its powerful serpentine tendrils. This vine is called the Strangler, and the mountain, the Chihuandassi, or, Table Of The Dead Men.

Ah, fascinating seems the Mountain,
 Clad in Morning's gold array !
Up, past many a silver fountain,
 Through cacti thorny,—o'er boulders gray,—
I slowly press, the weird, dread mesa scaling:
 I pause and upward gaze.
Far, far above in Heaven an eagle sailing
Shrieks, as if some untoward fate bewailing.
O'er the cliff's jagged brow a vine is trailing;
 As if wind-tossed, it sways.

Suddenly an unspeakable terror
 Thrills—chills my bosom's core !
Those marvellous tales deemed but the breath of Error—
 Mere superstitious lore—
Tales of this Height recur with ten-fold power,
 To haunt my quickened soul !
How silent—how oppressive is the hour!
No errant breeze sporteth with leaf or flower;
No bird-song floats from any adjacent bower.
 I near, at length, the goal.

'Tis reached!   My wayward heart controlling,
    I look!—What greeteth me?
Lo, yonder—rolling—rolling—rolling—
    Seems a tempestuous sea!
O, Thou to whom my spirit yields devotion!
    In dread I call to Thee!
The Vine!—The Vine!—The Strangler! 'Tis in motion
Far, far and wide, in waves like those of Ocean!
Tow'rd me 'tis surging—'tis no groundless notion!
    I turn—I haste— I flee!

Ah, Peak mysterious!   Dead Men's Table,
    Where bleacheth many a skull!
Thou art, indeed, no dream, no fable,
    The credulous to gull!
Round many a form those iron tendrils wreathing
    Have clung till life was past!
That living tide is round me swirling, seething,
My limbs those merciless coils will soon be sheathing!
One effort more! —more freely I am breathing—
    Thank God!- Safe!—Safe at last!

IF WE WILL.

We may walk, if we will, in sadness,
    With dark and downcast eye;
We may walk, if we will, in gladness,
    With scarce a sorrowful sigh.
To mourn forever is madness!
Look up to the orient sky!

— ‥

THE DYING DAY.

The day is slowly dying.   In the west
    Softly fade sunset's hues so bright, so gay;
    The sky hath purple grown—anon 'tis gray.
Afar on the horizon's rolling crest
Light struggles now with darkness.   O'er earth's breast
    The victor's car rolls on its trackless way;
    Night, sombre Night, holds now her silent sway:
Gladly the toiler welcomes well-won rest.
The day is dead, the summer day is dead—
    The day so full of promise at its birth!
        What hath it brought, O, love, to thee and me?
Ah, rapidly its sunny moments sped!
    With them came joys and hopes of countless worth—
        Hopes of fresh joys in glorious days to be!

BUNKER HILL MONUMENT.

It tells of heroes who bled and died
  In the holy cause of Freedom there;
And we point with never-dying pride
  To that lofty shaft as it soars in air!

It tells of patriotism pure—
  Of love for the land so nobly won.
O, may that love in our hearts endure,
  And our country endure while shines the sun!

Majestic structure! forever tower—
  In never-fading grandeur rise!
A warning to tyrants thou art each hour—
  A blessed memorial to our eyes!

VIVE LA REPUBLIQUE!

How many knaves have scourged and misruled men—
Knaves, undisguised by purple robe and crown!
With God-like air and fiend-like withering frown,
Wresting from Freedom's grasp both sword and pen,
They made earth one vast prison:—yea, and when
Fair Virtue's peerless flowers were trampled down—
Then did they laugh as laughs the ignoble clown,
And mock at Justice o'er and o'er again.
Despots! your day of glory has gone by!
In this great Land hath Liberty free voice;
She speaks to Man, and all that breathe can hear.
Soon shall all thrones, however proudly high,
From earth be swept:—all nations shall rejoice,
And Freedom be triumphant far and near.

WHEN WE WERE YOUNG.

O, the skies were bluer, brighter,
    Sweeter songs by the birds were sung,
And our hearts were so much lighter,
    Long ago, when we were young!
How slowly the days crept onward ever!
We deemed that age could reach us never,
    And we dreamed not that Hope had a siren's tongue!

Ah, how little we knew of sorrow!
    Ah, how little we knew of care!
Golden always seemed the morrow;
    Never a burden had we to bear!
Life went on like a pleasant story;
We had dreams of bliss, we had visions of glory,
    We were strong and eager to do and dare!

Alas! how swiftly the years are flying!
    Life seems now but a wearisome race;
Careworn, often sorrowing, sighing,
    We follow Hope in an endless chase.
Full many a prize we seek and capture;
But where is the grandeur, where the rapture
    That filled our hearts at the starting place?

PRESS ON!

———

Press on! Do doubts and fears oppress thee?
　Are strength and courage almost gone?
Do trials manifold distress thee?
　Press on—press boldly on!

Press on! Let Hope forsake thee never!
　Darkness shall flee and day shall dawn:
Success awaits thee! Forward ever!
　Press on—press boldly on!

Seek'st thou wealth?—Fame?—Truth's heavenly
　　　fountain—
　Wouldst thou a wreath of triumph don?
Shrink not, however steep the mountain:
　Press on—press boldly on!

Press on! Pause not with indecision
　Till opportunity be gone;
The longed-for goal shall glad thy vision:
　Press on—press boldly on!

THE OUTLAW.

—

He lurks amid the forest black;
Death is forever on his track—
Is near—is round him everywhere—
And evermore he must beware.

Ah! by that merciless hand hath blood
Full often flowed—a reeking flood!
Why should the Messenger so grim
Seem dread—seem hideous unto him?

Peace is a stranger to that breast;
Never is love therein a guest:
He knoweth not the joys of home;
A fugitive ever he must roam.

An outraged world he hath defied,
And striveth from its wrath to hide;   .
With Earth—with Heaven he long hath warred,
And is by all that breathe abhorred.

A price upon his head is set.
With no compunction—no regret—
He hath sent many to the tomb.—
Hath he not merited such doom?

E'en Midnight's sable, silent hour
To soothe his spirit scarce hath power;
His slumbers teem with dreams of strife:
His days with numberless fears are rife.

Hunted like some dread beast of prey,
Fiercely at last he turns at bay—
Battling most desperately doth fall,
And dieth execrating all.

LINES TO THE NEW YEAR.

Welcome, O, sweetly-smiling bright New Year!
Bring us fresh benisons from the hand of Him
Who bids the years with their mutations roll!
Some tears I drop upon the dead Year's bier,
But greet thee with a hope which naught can dim,—
With resolute heart, and with undaunted soul.

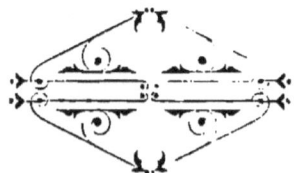

IN FEBRUARY.

Still a thick mantle of snow obscures Earth's breast,
  And Heaven is veiled with clouds of sombre gray;
  Still the fierce North-wind holds relentless sway:
Still are the streams with icy bonds oppressed;
The forest, still bare, hath no winged songful guest—
  Still, still the sweet-voiced birds remain away.
  Alas! when will the balmy South-wind play,   .
And Earth with sun, flowers, verdure, song be blest?
Patience, sad heart! there will be brighter hours!
The landscape will be green, the welkin blue;
Soft fragrance-laden airs will sweetly blow:
Streams will be free; woods gay; there will be flowers;
Glad birds their strains of rapture will renew:
Heaven will be cloudless, earth be all aglow!

                           .

THE SILENT CITY.

A wondrous city! Marvellously white
  Are all its mansions, palaces and towers.
  Oblivion here is throned 'mid rarest flowers,
And here the day is silent as the night.
Mindless alike of darkness and of light—
  Foul weather or fair—sweet sunshine or bleak showers—
  Of all that passes in this world of ours—
The dwellers slumber, noting not Time's flight.
Lo! on an obelisk of snow-white stone
  A raven gloomily sits, but gives no sound.
    Streets, avenues, squares are voiceless and untrod.
None wake to sigh, and none in slumber moan.
  In rayless halls, the multitudes around
    Dreamless await the wakening voice of God.

ODE TO YOSEMITE FALLS.

Dash on, O, Cataract, in thy might!
Leap, leap from yon stupendous height
To the Vale below—most glorious sight!—

Down—down—forever down—
Rush from the steep's Titanic crown,
O'er cliffs that, awe-inspiring, frown!

Soaring prey-birds bathe their wings—
Exultant—free—most fearless things!—
In the spray thy torrent flings—

As, skirting the precipice, they seek
An ærie on some distant peak—
And in thee oft dip thirsty beak.

Night and day—forevermore—
Making a most thunderous roar,
Thy vast libation thou dost pour—

An offering unto Him whose Hand
So fashioned thee—at whose command
Arose these heights so huge and grand!

O, how magnificent thou art!
With enraptured soul and heart,
I gaze—and fain would not depart!

Full many thus have stood by thee;
Full many thy glories yet shall see,
In years—in centuries to be; –

Full many a bard shall on thee gaze,
And, enchanted, yield thee praise,
In sublime and soulful lays.

Mighty Cascade! with joy I bring
To thee a poet's offering;—
Accept the heart-felt song I sing!

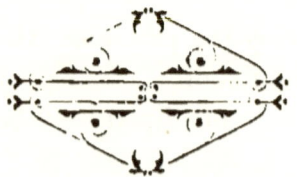

EVENING.

O, Vesper Hour! thy loveliness I prize!
  Thy peaceful scenes I passionately love!
    A world of poetry I find in thee,
O, Evening!—in thy crimson and violet skies,
  In thy tranquility below, above!
    What beautiful thoughts thou dost suggest to me!

SWEET MOON, SILVER MOON.

Sweet Moon, silver Moon,
   Sailing through the skies,
Softly shine, O, softly shine
   Where my loved one slumb'ring lies!
Though o'er her couch thy radiance streams,
She wakes not to behold thy beams;
Thou canst not charm her with thy gleams:
   Closed forever are her eyes.
Softly shine, O, argent Moon,
   Where asleep my loved one lies.

Sweet Moon, silver Moon,
   Sinking in the west,
Gently throw thy parting beams
   Where my loved one lies at rest.
Gently pierce the churchyard's gloom;
Gently touch the flowers that bloom
On the green turf of her tomb——
   Kiss the sod above her breast:
Mildly beam, O, waning Moon,
   On my loved one's place of rest.

SYMPATHY.

As falls the rain on the thirsty land,
  On the withering grass and the drooping flowers,
As falls the sunshine soft and bland
  On the grateful earth after night's bleak hours;
So, in vine-wreathed cot, or in princely halls,
  Wherever Sorrow has thrown a dart,
A word of heart-felt sympathy falls
  On a wounded, bleeding heart.

Has a soul's bright hope been swept away,
  Even as a leaf on a wintry blast?
Is a spirit that once was sunny and gay
  By affliction's darksome cloud o'ercast?
By sympathy let thy heart be stirred;
  O, haste to give, if thou canst, relief!
Though it cost thee naught, a kindly word
  Will lighten a load of grief.

Let thy mission forever be,
  Where'er thou art—where'er thou may'st go—
The world from pain and sorrow to free,
  To waken joy and banish woe.
With words of comfort—sweet rays of gold—
  Dispel life's clouds, wheresoever they frown;
Heaven will requite thee with bliss untold,
  And award thee a priceless crown.

AT REST.

"There remaineth therefore a rest."

The eyes are closed, they will see no more
The changeful scenes of this earthly shore;
The hands are folded—their tasks are o'er—
They will move no more, till within Heaven's door
     They strike a glad harp 'mid the Blest:
The feet that were once so busy are still,
No longer they tread paths thorny and chill;
They will walk no more, no more, until
They wander o'er fadeless vale and hill,
     In the World where the weary rest.

A wasted form, once fair and proud,
Slumbers, wrapt in a snow-white shroud;
The spirit, with mystic wings endowed,
Hath sped beyond the farthest cloud,
     Unfettered, unoppressed:
Earth could not keep the tired soul;
Free from mortal care and control,
In a measureless flight it hath sought its Goal,
Where, while uncounted ages roll,
     The weary are at rest.

Life's manifold trials at length are past,
Life's heavy burdens aside are cast:
Life's hopes and fears are ended at last.
Ne'er, ne'er shall Misfortune's merciless blast
  Break the peace of that motionless breast.
O, Father of All! in thy Home on high,
Thou hearest every anguished cry,
Each moan of pain, each bitter sigh.
Thou biddest Care and Sorrow fly,
  And givest the weary rest.

THE RETURN OF SPRING.

Lo, Winter hath relaxed his icy clasp!
  The heavens display a brighter, fresher blue,
    And Nature smiles once more in quiet gladness!
Ah! soon will flowers spring up to meet our grasp;
  Soon will the landscape wear its emerald hue,
    And hours of joy atone for hours of sadness.

THE BROOKLET.

Thou com'st from the pine-clothed mountain,
  Down through the rock-strewn glen,
Making most beautiful music
  For the ears of weary men.

Thou warblest songs enchanting—
  Songs that reach the heart—
Lays far surpassing in sweetness
  The proudest strains of Art;—

Songs of rest for the burdened,
  Of solace for the sad,
Of hope for the gloomy and downcast,
  And pæans for the glad.

Thy noble mission is endless;
  Unceasingly, night and day,
Thou carol'st in sweet contentment,
  As thou hastenest on thy way.

Through sweet and cool recesses
  Thou rapidly windest down,
Till at length thou placidly stealest
  Through the lovely and pleasant town;

Then deepening, broadening ever,
  Serenely thou glidest afar,
Reflecting the tranquil heavens,
  And sun and moon and star.

Like thine, O, silver Brooklet,
  May my life's current flow
Melodiously and sweetly,
  A blessing to all below;

May it deepen and broaden ever,
  Unsullied, like to thee,
Till, a noble, majestic river,
  It shall reach Eternity's Sea.

NEVER DESPAIR.

O, thou who art with sorrow bowed,
  Despair not! Cease thy dreary repining!
Have hope! Beyond grief's darkest cloud,
  The sun of gladness is sweetly shining!
Though the storm be wrathful, wild and loud,
  Keep heart, and watch for the Silver Lining!

THE CHANGEABLE FLOWER.

Botanists have recently made a remarkable discovery in Tehuantepec, Mexico, establishing the fact that the native "Hinta" has a flower that changes its color three times a day in favorable weather. At morning it is white, at noon it is red, at evening it is blue. This extraordinary blossom emits its perfume only two hours out of every twenty-four- from 11 A. M. to 1 P. M.

At morn 'tis white as the beautiful snow,
When it falls from Heaven to Earth below—
When in stainless mantle it wraps the globe—
White—Oh! white as an angel's robe!

At noontide a gorgeous garb it wears;
Deepest red is the hue it bears—
'Tis red as the wine-cup's ruddy glow,
Ay, red as the life-tide's crimson flow.

At eve it hath an azure hue;
'Tis sweetly—O, divinely blue!—
Blue as some Beauty's witching eye,
Blue as the cloudless heavens on high.

Sweet is the breath of that marvellous flower;
But not in every passing hour,
Upon the circumambient air,
It wafts around its fragrance rare.

As midday approaches, its exquisite scent,
Sweeter, methinks, for being long pent,
Grateful to every passer-by,
Is borne abroad on the soft wind's sigh.

When the dazzling splendor of noonday dies,
And the sun doth pass to western skies,
That delicate odor none may inhale.—
On the morrow again 'twill lade the gale.

Bloom on, lovely flower, in thy Southern land,
Kissed by breezes balmy and bland !
A bard in the North-land, far away,
As a tribute to thee, breathes forth this lay.

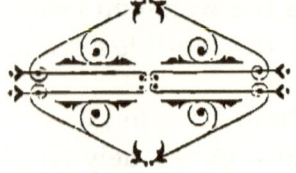

THE CYCLONE.

Serene was the earth and serene was the sky
From morning till midday—till midday passed by;
But ere in the west the bright day-orb sank down,
A muttering cloud rose with Stygian frown.

As the prey-bird descends on the quarry below—
As the condor descends on the dreamy-eyed doe—
As descends the bold eagle—as a demon in mirth—
So that cloud out of Heaven descended to earth.

Like an army all horrent with glittering spears,
So, arrayed in the glory and splendor of years,
A city with spires on an eminence stood,
Enwalled by a wide-spreading evergreen wood.

As the fierce lion bounds through the jungle before,
In the strength of his rage and the pride of his roar,
So that blackening cloud hurried out of the west,—
Like a hasty avenger it paused not for rest.

And the cedars were bowed like the vassals that fling
Their faces to earth when approached by their king,
And that city so stately, so far-famed, so proud—
Ah, that queenly-throned city was lost in the cloud.

And the Heaven-reaching tower, from summit to base,
In a moment was shattered like some broken vase;
Mansions, palaces, temples were crushed and down-hurled,
And their fragments like leaves tossed by autumn-gusts
  whirled.

And the maiden who waited the hour to be bride,—
And the youth buoyant-hearted with hope undenied,—
And the snowy-haired pair—young and old—sad and gay—
On the Wind-fiend's dark pinions were borne far away.

And bare is the face of that eminence now,
And furrowed for aye is its garlandless brow,
And they whose abodes proudly crested that steep
Dwell no more amid mortals—ah, lowly they sleep!

THE HERMIT.

Upon yon mountain's side a hermit dwells,
Self-prisoned, self-exiled from the haunts of men,
Like some wild animal in a darksome den.
Few sounds, save those from far-off village bells,
Float thither from the ambient world.   Where wells
A green-fringed fount, whose streamlet threads yon glen,
At times he strays, but, if perceived, again
He seeks his cavern—gloomiest of cells!
O, God! let me not live so drear a life!
Oft, oft let me behold the face of Man—
Of lovely Woman!—Let me often hear
The human voice, with kindly accents rife;
Let me have friends with smiles to cheer life's span,
And let me die with loved ones lingering near!

THE WEST-WIND.

Softly the west-wind o'er the landscape sighs,
  Bearing the fragrance of a thousand flowers—
  Rustling the foliage of a thousand bowers.
Softly it fans the cheek—softly it dies;
Gently anon it doth once more arise:
  Delicate blossoms on the earth it showers;
  'Mid the tall forest which so proudly towers,
In murmurs to the song-birds it replies.
Wind of the West! still wander o'er earth's breast,
  Sweet as a breath wafted from Paradise—
    Light as the pressure of an angel's hand!
Whisper to all of quietude and rest—
  Of all things peaceful 'neath these halcyon skies—
    Of all things beautiful, of all things bland!

TWILIGHT.

When o'er the earth, with dewy mantle,
　She comes, what thoughts of home
And all the loving dear ones there assembled
　Arise in those who roam!

Ever she brings us recollections
　Of glad and bright days past—
Days that shall live in our remembrance alway—
　Yea, long as life shall last!

Ever she bringeth tender mem'ries
　Of those whose days are o'er—
Visions of those whom we shall fondly welcome
　'Mid earthly scenes no more!

O, moments sacred to reflection—
　To memory and love—
That move the heart to sweet and gentle feeling,
　And lift the soul above!

Ah, 'tis a time for solemn musing,
　And not for thoughtless mirth—
To view the Past and all its vanished glories—
　When Twilight steals o'er earth!

WITHIN THE HARBOR.

The deep is white with rage!   Ah! what strong barque
  Could for the space of but one fleeting hour
  Brave the wroth element's demoniac power?
No stars illumine Heaven; 'tis dark—all dark—
Save when the lightning sharply flashes:—hark!
  How loud the breakers' roar!   From its high tower,
  The light-house beacon gleams through the fierce shower,
Athwart the sea, a flickering, faint spark!
Outside the Harbor, all is dread and wild!
Within, how sweetly are the ships at rest,
No matter though 'tis dark below, above!
So, when life's ocean turbulent grows, God's child
Reposes, with a calm, untroubled breast,
Within the Harbor of Almighty Love.

THE SUNNY SIDE.

Look not on the dark side of life,
  For the sunny side always is best.
Be brave in the glorious strife!
  Let Cheerfulness dwell in thy breast.

Mourn not for the hopes that were crossed
  By some petty misfortune or ill;
There are others which may not be lost:
  Though earnest, wait patiently still.

Walk not in the darkness of doubt
  When Truth beameth brightly and clear:
Let not thy faith's lamp be put out:
  Despair not—a Helper is near.

There are shadows that come ev'rywhere,
  To dim the sunlight of the soul,
And life's burdens we all have to bear,
  For they are beyond our control:

There are woes that fill ev'ry heart,
  And make dreary the pathways of men,
But the gloom of grief will depart,
  And the brightness of joy come again.

O, let us not walk in the dark!
  Let us trust in the Father above,
The bow of His promise mark,
  And bask in the sun of His love.

AT MORNING.

Lo, morning in beauty
  Now dawns upon earth!
Awaken to duty!
  A new day has birth.
Birds full of gladness
  Are voicing their glee;
They banish all sadness,
  And why should not we?

O, whence is thy sorrow?
  Those tears—whence are they?
Do fears for to-morrow
  Make darksome to-day?
Birds full of gladness
  Are voicing their glee;
They borrow no sadness,
  And pray why should we?

A SONG OF THE SEA.

Beautiful Sea! Majestic Sea!
Ever changeful—forever free !
In grandeur what is like to thee?
Thou smilest in innocuous glee,
  When kissed by the sunlight golden and warm,
And anon thou art wrathful as aught can be,
  When over thee sweeps the furious storm !
In sublimity what can rival thee,
Everlasting unmeasured, unfathomed Sea !

Mighty Sea! Glorious Sea!
How gayly the ships go forth on thee!
But thou canst deceptive and ruthless be—
Yea, e'en as that creature beneath thy waves,
  Which seemeth to be a beautiful flower,
Till whatsoever as prey it craves
  Is fully within its grasp of power. *
Oft, oft thou art treacherous, O, Sea!
To those who trustingly voyage on thee.

Endless Sea! Eternal Sea!
When all who with rapture now gaze on thee
  Shall view thee no more—shall cease to be—
Thou wilt roll as ever thou hast since God
  Formed thy boundaries with His Hand.
And men o'er thy billows will go abroad,
  And thou wilt by turns be boist'rous and bland—
Evermore thou wilt be as changeful and free,
Sempiternal measureless, fathomless Sea!

*The opelet.

YESTERDAY AND TO-DAY.

Yesterday's gone with its sorrows and pleasures—
Departed—lost in Eternity's Sea!
Its sad or glad measures, its losses and treasures
  No more shall elate or depress you and me—
  Yesterday's gone like the clouds that flee.

To-day the sun is resplendently shining;
  Heaven benignly shows its blue!
All fears resigning, cease fruitless repining!
  To-day hath treasures for me and for you—
  To-day our sublimest hopes may prove true.

MY OLD HOME.

In dreams—sweet dreams—I oft revisit thee,
  Dear home, nestling 'mid trees so far away;
  And as in childhood's happy hours of play—
Ah, sunny hours of incomparable glee!—
I tread the old paths, buoyant, blithesome, free!
  Again earth seems to me a Paradise gay—
  An Age of Gold each swiftly-passing day!
Cares, doubts and fears like sombre shadows flee.
I see the sunshine gild thee as of old,
  I feel the fragrant winds that round thee sigh;
    I wander 'mid the green fields as of yore!
I waken—other scenes mine eyes behold:
  Those fancies—blissful fancies!—fade and die—
    Alas! I am a careworn man once more.

WHERE IS MY YOUTH?

Gone like the fragrance of a perished rose,
  Gone like the sunshine of a vanished day,
  Gone like a leaf by wild winds swept away;
Gone like the pure flakes of departed snows,
Gone like a beautiful dream at slumber's close,
  Gone, gone, alas! forever and for aye!
  Dead are its joys! Its visions—where are they?
Ah! youth but once comes—once forever goes!
O, youth, sweet youth! O, ever-sunny youth!
  Hast thou departed, never to return?
    Are thy glad days with all their pleasures o'er?
Ah me, ah me! 'tis sober, sober truth!
  Though for thine hours even in dreams I yearn,
  They come no more, alas! they come no more!

THE OLD SCHOOL-HOUSE.

Rank grasses wave where erst it stood;
    The place is desolate and lone:
    All who assembled here have grown
To manhood or to womanhood.

Once more I see, with memory's eyes,
    The children as of yore at play;
    In fancy I am young and gay,
With spirit cloudless as the skies.

Ah! vanished are those early days!
    Departed is life's golden morn;
    New pleasures and new hopes are born,
But cherished are youth's haunts and ways.

Some who with light feet pressed this spot
    Will tread the paths of earth no more;
    For them life's lessons all are o'er—
Its tasks and all its cares forgot.

The flowers blow, the grass is green,
    Around my childhood Idol's tomb:
    For her the flowers unfading bloom—
The flowers but by Immortals seen.

Not far away the brooklet flows,
    Where, with a fresh and wild delight,
    Full oft we gathered lilies white
And stainless as untrodden snows.

Near by the willows stand, whose shade,
  When summer noons poured down their rays,
  Gave shelter from the sun's fierce blaze.
What garlands of their boughs we made!

Lo, yonder is the well-loved slope,
  Where, when keen Winter heaped his snow,
  We coasted—cheek and soul aglow—
Buoyant with peerless mirth and hope.

Still smiles enchantingly the vale,
  In robe of verdure gayly dressed,
  Where we were wont to rove in quest
Of the sweet violet meek and pale.

Ah, loved old structure! thou art gone!
  Within thy time-worn walls no more
  Shall young souls gather earthly lore—
No more the needful lesson con.

Naught here attracts the stranger's gaze;
  Naught marvellous the eye can see;
  Yet 'tis enchanted ground to me,
Hallowed by memories of old days.

Still, as the swift years come and go,
  And time on all things leaves its trace,
  This aye shall seem a sacred place—
Yea, long as life shall last below.

SUMMER AND AUTUMN.

Summer, like a faded belle,
  Heavy-hearted,
Hath regretfully bidden us farewell,
  And departed.

Autumn, like a gay coquette,
  Forward rushes,
And strives to enchant us and make us forget
  Summer's blushes.

SONGS OF THE GOLDEN-ROD.

I.

A thousand miniature suns
  Illuminate my way—
Golden flowers of the golden-rod,
  Bright as the orb of day!

Shine, lovely luminaries,—
  Still shine!—Still softly nod,
O, Autumn's most enchanting flower—
  Beautiful golden-rod!

II.

Autumn! what wealth thou bringest!
  Wherever thou hast trod,
We behold what Man so covets—
  Gold -- the gold of the golden-rod!

Why need we probe earth's bosom
  In quest of glittering ore?
Gold!   Gold! 'tis all around us!--
  And do we seek for more?

III.

Lo! fringing the russet woodland,
  And the meadows bare and brown,
Waves the majestic golden-rod,
  Brighter than kingly crown!

In vast, far-reaching masses--
  How splendid to behold!--
Wind-swept, it rolls in billows--
  A marvellous sea of gold!

LOST YOUTH.

Age is weary, age is dreary!
  Oh! could'st thou at will recall
The days of youth, so bright, so cheery,
  Would'st thou not relinquish all—
All thy hoarded earthly treasures—
All thy long-sought empty pleasures?
  But canst thou do it?—Never!
Youth once past is gone forever!

Thou may'st search o'er vale and mountain—
  O'er all the world—'tis sombre truth—
But thou ne'er canst find the fountain
  Renowned of old—the Fount of Youth!
Futile were such quest—'twere madness—
Naught can e'er restore youth's gladness;
  Thou canst recall it never!
Youth once past is gone forever!

ONLY IN DREAMS.

Only in dreams we meet again,
  As young and gay—as buoyant-hearted—
As fond and hopeful and happy as when
  We met in those days so long departed!
Only in dreams I see her face,
Bright with a smile of the old-time grace, —
  Only in dreams—sweet dreams!

Only in dreams her voice I hear,
  So soft and gentle, so sweet and low, —
As melodious, silvery and clear —
  As thrilling as in the Long Ago!
Only in dreams her eloquent eyes,
Cerulean as the Summer skies,
  Reply to mine—only in dreams.

Thus only we meet beneath the tree,
  Under whose boughs so oft we met
When eve made halcyon land and sea;—
  Ah, moments my soul can ne'er forget!
Only in dreams our lips unite—
Love's holy seal—ah, only in bright
  And unforgotten dreams!

Only in Dreamland, side by side,
　We stray together, as of yore,
Where softly-rippling waters glide.
　She walks—white-robed—another shore—
The Shore of Heaven's gorgeous golden Sea
She walks with seraphs, who walks with me
　Only in dreams—in dreams.

O, Earth! how dark thou seem'st—how drear—
　When I awake to thy sounds and sights!
O, Land whose skies are always clear—
　Where years have no winters—days no nights!
When shall I tread thy marvellous Shore,
With her whom I behold no more,
　Save in dreams—only in dreams?

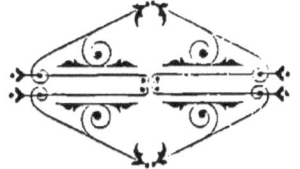

A SEPTEMBER IDYL.

No sullen clouds mar the unfading
    Expanse on high:
A restful quiet is pervading
    Earth, sea and sky.
Gay colors doth the forest wear;
Crimson leaves glow here and there,
Golden ones float everywhere.
Delicious coolness hath the air,
    For this is golden September —
    Beautiful golden September!

Vanished are Summer's brilliant hours;
    Her songsters gay
Have ceased their songs; her gorgeous flowers—
    Where, where are they?
Gone—all are gone! but who will cast
Looks of regret on bright days past,
While days so calm, so halcyon last,
And all the splendors that thou hast,
    O, golden September?—
    Beautiful golden September!

THE RUINED PALACE.

Here once was Royalty in all its glory!
　What splendor was consigned to moth and rust!
　He who here swayed a sceptre sleeps in dust:
The warrior-princes fell in battles gory.
The rent walls silently relate a story
　Of past magnificence and pomp.　Here lust
　Of power and pride were rife!　The scornful gust
Flouts the huge mass.—Ah, all is transitory!
Once gorgeous structure! thou art but as all
　Man's edifices shall become at last!
　　Stupendous pile, doomed to inanity!
Even as I tread this echoing desolate hall,
　I hear a voice heard in an age long past,
　　Solemnly saying, "All is vanity!"

AT LAST.

When the dark clouds of Winter
　　Obscure the sweet skies,
And the heavenly azure
　　No more glads our eyes,
One solace is ours,
　　'Mid storm and blast;
We know lovely Spring
　　Will come—at last.

At last the drear clouds
　　Will vanish away,
And Heaven will smile
　　All the livelong day;
Earth's garment of snow
　　Will aside be cast,
And lily and rose
　　Will bloom—at last.

When we pine 'mid the Winter
　　Of earthly woe,
And blasts are bitter
　　And clouds hang low,
Hope softly whispers:
　　·· 'Twill soon be past;
Joy's radiant Spring-time
　　Will come—at last."

At last the trials　　　　　　　•
　　That vex the soul
Like the clouds so darksome
　　Away will roll—

Will be lost as the clouds are
  In sky-depths so vast.
We shall dwell in the sunshine
  Of gladness—at last.

At last all the sorrows
  Of life will cease;
At last all life's tumult
  Will end in peace:
The years—weary years—
  Are flying fast,
And rest—perfect rest—
  Will come—at last.

At last we shall slumber
  In dreamless beds,
And roses will blossom
  Above our heads;
Whether skies be bright
  Or overcast,
We shall sleep—sweetly sleep—
  At last—at last.

At last all the noble
  Whose lives accord
With Heaven's blessed Canons
  Will have reward;
In splendor fadeless
  And unsurpassed,
The God-crowned holy
  Shall shine—AT LAST.